The AVENUE of REGRETTABLE FAREWELLS

avenue des adieux regrettables

a novelette

Venus De Mileage

THE AVENUE OF REGRETTABLE FAREWELLS

Published in the United Kingdom
Copyright © Venus De Mileage
2014

All rights reserved. No part of this publication may be
reproduced, stored in a retrieval system, or transmitted
in any form or by any means, electronic, mechanical,
photocopying, recording or otherwise, without the prior
written permission of the publisher.

This book is undedicated.

Because it was always going to be goodbye.

"Silence be the stranger and the strangler too,
of tongues that never kiss nor speak.
The tongues of me and you."

I
L'AVENUE
where the aches of hearts govern

The Avenue of Regrettable Farewells is situated beyond a corner as yet unturned. A corner of a street; a street that is, in its mad fusion of brazen modern attitude and ancient architecture, much like any other street that houses shops whose windows offer untold treasures for strangely shaped and even ill-gotten coins. Technically, it might be supposed, the 'street' out of which the 'avenue' runs tributary, is more an avenue than the avenue itself, but where myth and whispers and the aches of hearts govern, there is no place for technicality. And as this avenue, this living graveyard of goodbyes, boasts no postal address and claims no place on any geographical map, it can be named an avenue or a lane or whatsoever it or anyone, for that matter, wishes; for who can dispute the details of that which does not exist for everyone and does not, when it does exist, manifest itself in identical ways in the eyes of the beholders? The avenue, like beauty, is indefinable. Like love, it is intangible. Like death, it is just around a corner as yet unturned.

II
LA VILLE DE GRIS
the principal metropolis

The street from which the avenue branches is a street in The City of Grey. It could be your city, or mine, in this country or that – any principal metropolis made up of ominous nephilimic structures which shrink men in both stature and spirit, swallow them and stifle them with air that is not real; air that hisses like chambered killer gas deep in the bodies of the buildings.

The temptation might be to call these innards of these buildings bellies or bowels, but they are more like the *vasa deferentia* in places such as these. Let us think, for argument's sake, of a concrete tower which rises like a monstrous and inordinately proud cock. Its intrusive exhibitionist form and shadow thrusts upward, fucking the sky and skyline, impregnating the city with dirty money shot out like filthy cum - full in the façades of other buildings, fullsting ahead in their grimed window eyes. The city is grown of stone and steel over years, risen – illuminated, stalagmitesque - made by man, by human mind and hand, its demanding flashy-flashing sluttish signage, impatient growling hooting vehicles and alluring shop window treasures are all brightly coloured and brightly lit, but it is a place, in sentiment, that can only be grey, for to work here or submit and be a starch-collared slave to it, a man or woman, by necessity, must become a bloodless shadow of their dream self, even, their real self. Grey as steel and stone. Who knows which of the man or woman is the true being?

III
MAN

Andre Guillermo was a man who had decided to turn from golden to grey, and while for the sake of his protection he wears the mask of a pseudonym, you will recognize him instantly because we all know or know of someone like him, someone who has turned grey by choice. It is not that his hair was the cooled-ash white of steel, or that any aspect of him physically or in spirit was grey, such as grey is. In fact, Andre Guillermo was something of a striking figure – not the sort of man who usually goes overlooked or blends into the background.

To truly become a part of the City of Grey, Andre Guillermo would first have to say goodbye to things that would, for their vibrancy and brilliance, be obstacles to his achieving the greyness that he now, or at least in this particular moment of particular peculiarity, believed he desired. And to make final this lamentable departure from the beautiful and dazzling aspects of his self that he intended to cast off he would have to turn a corner. That corner. The one that was as yet unturned. The corner of the street from which The Avenue of Regrettable Farewells runs tributary.

Andre had decided that in order to live, he must die, die the very worst of deaths, the half death. He must let the vampire city parch his veins, his spirit. The half-death leaves the body and the mind intact - functioning, automaton, - but submits to an undug unmarked infertile grave the suicided soul and an overnight bag filled with dreams pencilled in for discarding. It was with such a bag as this, meticulously packed, zipped, buckled tight and strapped, like a burdensome child, on the wearied slope of his back, that Andre Guillermo set off for the Avenue of Regrettable Farewells.

Of course, he was sure he had never been there before; sure that he had only heard rumours of its existence, mostly in his head. Sometimes eavesdropped word had come his way, when people spoke in weighty tones, not of their own experiences of the Avenue, but of thirdhand tales, twisted out of shape and recognition, told but warped in the retelling, of friends of friends' friends who had, as Andre now intended to, partially defected from life.

Nothing is for sale in the shops on The Avenue of Regrettable Farewells, although the window displays are always intriguing. Goodbyes, hated though they often are, command no price, sentiment cannot be bought and sold. In any case, Andre Guillermo, would take no money with him, so should he be enamoured of or by the objects in the shop windows he passed on the avenue, he had nothing, so he thought, with which to barter.

You might think that to transport oneself to the Avenue of Regrettable Farewells one must be practiced in magic or meditation, or have what is sometimes sneeringly described as an overactive imagination. But this is not the rule, if there can be rules. On the contrary, the will to discard supposed whimsy is often all that is needed to lead people there. Throw even the smallest dream away, toss into the city's river a fledgling aspiration to become whatever one might secretly, warmly, hope to become, weigh down that little flightless wishboned bird with the deadweight burden of words like 'delusion', and terms like 'pipe dream' and you have drowned your desires in dark waters and when they sink, traceless, down into the wetsmoke sludge that even the prettiest silver rivers dress their beds with, a part of the soul sinks and dies too. A seemingly inconsequential action like that can secure you a ticket to the Avenue of Regrettable Farewells, or an unwritten map of the whereabouts of this sad

sad quarter.

Andre Guillermo had given up hope, as others give up cigarettes or alcohol or gambling - determinedly. To hope, he thought, simply made you vulnerable to disappointment, to hurt. And hope, aspiration, all the elusive things, were a distraction. He wanted them gone.

Regrettable farewell.

IV

LA PREMIÈRE FENÊTRE

of the pointlessness of tears

Most who enter the Avenue of Regrettable Farewells, by whatever means, notice the sounds first rather than the sights. Usually it's the weeping, soft though it is, that is heard above other noises, noises that are not humanborn. And, seeking the source of this haunting lamentation the eye is drawn to a shop front with a bay window, much like the sort nostalgic recollection gives toy shops; a window made up of small panes of unclear glass, framed in oak that is damp and home to industrious wood boring creatures that in a setting less surreal than this would eat the structure clean away. But here, on the Avenue of Regrettable Farewells all things are in a state of aimless perpetuality; no journeys seem to conclude, not a single destination is ever reached, and so a pointless termite's purpose is as lost as a lost person's. All non-culminating experience is captured, as if looped on film, in the lenses of the windows.

In this bay window, from where the weeping sound originates, is a woman, naked, kneeling on a tiled floor, her head not quite wept away completely, who unseeing and rocking, folds toward a neat pool of milk so white, yet deliciously pearlescent, it might have been drawn or leaked from the swollen everfull breast of a goddess. Were it not for the ectoplasmic shroud that shrouds the weeping woman's head, you might think she had no head at all. Like a sheet thrown over a ghost to reveal or perhaps illuminate its shape, this pale cowl, which made Andre Guillermo think suddenly and painfully of Magritte's faceless masked lovers, seemed at once to give its wearer both an identity and an intriguing but morbid sense of anonymity. As she rocks and dips forward the observer might be forgiven for thinking she wants to lap at the pool of cream with a thirsty dedicated cat-like tongue. Seeing her there in this attitude that suggests an erotic and yet reverent supplication, such thoughts are perhaps more sexual wish than predictable expectation. But she will not bend to lick. She does not weep for hunger. She weeps in regret. She will do only what the Avenue allows. She will cry unending proverbial tears over the spilled milk of the cheerless adage; a living embodiment, far more impactful in its being so sensual, so visual, of that weary cliché. But the spilled milk is solid, and not milk at all, it is a slab of parian, hard, non fluid, undrinkable. Nothing here is what or as it seems.

III
WOMAN

For reasons Andre Guillermo could not initially explain or fully understand he found the scene arousing in its sorrow and the woman's posture, something in that apparent willingness to submit, now revived a memory in him that erased the bagged heads of Magritte's lovers from view. Instead he was reminded that a woman had knelt before him once, in precisely such a manner of tender agreeable subservience; she had knelt at his feet as if to pray, but had not spoken a single word of worship. He had placed his hand upon her head, stroked her hair. It was not prayer her tongue tasted that day. This moment had taken place in a garden, a garden verdant and beautifully purposely neglected just as any of the gods might have intended. The garden had not been Andre Guillermo's garden. The woman had not been his wife.

VI
LA SECONDE FENÊTRE
of fate and fortune

In the next shop window Andre saw an upturned horseshoe that hung in mid air, beneath this seven rabbits' feet (complete with the sadistic blood-rusted traps that had trapped them) sat in the sickening sickle shape of their number. Without being conscious of his actions, Andre Guillermo felt in his trouser pockets for his wallet or for loose change. But why would he, or any man, even a man who had decided to turn grey as he had, wish to acquire such things, things that were so clearly a portent, a representation, of luck that had run out? The truth is, he would not, unless he harboured some notion of being able to possess things in order to change things, have command over them, unless he thought how powerful, how magickal it might be to set the horseshoe rightways-up, that it would no longer leak fortune, turning it from good to bad, from its uterine arc.

It occurred to Andre, as he sought coins that were not there in his empty pockets, that the horseshoe, despite its more obvious significance, was in some way a symbol of hope and he thought, If the luck is perpetually running out, if there is indeed an endless supply of luck to be lost, that means luck is a commodity which replenishes itself, organic matter that reseeds and regrows. Reseeds and regrows to grow and then… die?

This is how things work on the Avenue of Regrettable Farewells, the traveller must turn a corner to enter it, yet turn many more once there and turn many more again if ever they are to leave. Around every corner, is another corner, a corner as yet unturned.

In this uncharted landscape there are no signposts, but on the branches of leafless trees that grow from cracks in the buildings and from the tops of towers, kid gloves hang and point this way and that and send the traveller widdershins along his way. When a breeze blows, these gloves, these child-ghost hands, appear to be waving, and while the gesture might easily be one that says hello, on the Avenue of Regrettable Farewells the haunting gesticulation means only one thing. Goodbye.

Andre had begun to feel oddly guilty about leaving the faceless woman crying over the marble *laichespill*. He could still hear her but he followed the trees' pale pointing fingers and walked further along the avenue, noticing for the first time that it seemed to be night, albeit not the darkest of nights, and yet the sky was both moonless and starless. The only clear illumination was provided by street lamps that stood sentry at intervals along the way, but these beacons were dimmed by the black veils that each wore.

VII
THE WIDOWS' WALK

Andre said aloud, "Widows' Walk." He wondered where he had heard the words before, and thought of ships and Italianate architecture, then he wondered if he had actually ever heard the words before or if he had just that moment thought them up. The Avenue of Regrettable Farewells can do things to a man's mind and memory. Back in the city, the City of Grey, Andre would have typed the term and pressed buttons and searched for answers, or even, given his penchant for tradition, looked in a book for enlightenment. On the Avenue, no such line of enquiry could be taken, there were no devices from which solutions to riddles could be clicked or conjured and none of the books there, and there were, and are, many, would offer any written answers at all. At best they would simply raise more answerable questions.

VIII
LA TROISIÈME FENÊTRE
of books and burials

It was a shop that ostensibly presented itself as a bibliophile's haven that Andre came upon next. Through the window he saw thick and slim volumes, books which, he thought, might be antiquarian – their leather bindings, marbled paper and gilded spines suggested age. Thousands upon thousands of books stretched far back into the shop's dark dusty interior but this was no library, there was no cohesive cataloguing, no alphabetic system nor organization of subject matter, nor were all the books on shelves, for there was only one shelf, and on this a book sat solo; sprouting from its closed pages, as might a bookmark or bookworm, was a single flower, a flower as purple as a crazed poet's soul, and tied with twine to its stem, was a label upon which was written in an exacting hand the word *Erysimum.* The wallflower. It was this book that intrigued Andre, it was this book that Andre wanted most to read, despite there being bigger and more attractively packaged, more beautiful books in the shop. But there was something of despair and unpromise in those other editions. Each of the thousands and thousands of other books stood, as headstones do in graveyards, line upon line of them, some in deeper states of collapse into what Andre now noticed was grass and earth, rather than the more usual tile or wood floor of more usual shops.

"Are the authors dead? Is that what this means?" asked Andre. He had turned, while standing perfectly still, another of the Avenue's corners. Andre leaned forward and peered into the bookshop through the dirty window, and as far as his sight and the obstacles of lines of books obscuring lines of books would allow, he began to read the titles. He had never heard of any of these books. He looked for the authors' names, but there were none, the works were unattributed.

Why he should now be perplexed by the odd nature of the shops on the Avenue is a mystery all its own. He had been less so when he'd seen the weeping woman and the display of upturned horseshoe and rabbits' feet. But there was something about this bookshop - such as it was - something about this place that touched him.

The sign above the shop's door was written in French and read:

Cimetière Des Livres Inachevés

Andre, despite his name (which is not, as you know his real name) did not speak French. He knew but one French phrase, a blasphemous and dirty one, which he had learned years before and, having perfected its pronunciation, often used for mirthful effect. But one does not need fluency in French to understand the establishment's name and the nature of its window display.

"Are the authors dead?" asked Andre again.

It is not uncommon for visitors to the Avenue of Regrettable Farewells to progress and unprogress in this way. Andre Guillermo had turned a corner in asking the question in the first place, but to ask it again without at least attempting to answer it before doing so was a doubling back, of sorts. He shook his head. "No, no, that's not it, is it? That's not right," he said. "The books have died; or is it that they never lived? *Inachevés.* The books were never achieved? But why?"

Ah, another corner turned. Then…
"Did the authors die? Are the authors dead?"

…And back again. Andre Guillermo was a man circling himself, circling his own thought processes like a maniacal dog pointlessly pursuing its own crazy tail. An Ouroborus.

No author names. "No author names… because…why?"

Because… The biggest corner so far, but he had not turned it yet.

Andre tried the handle of the shop's door. He hadn't expected it to open but it did, with surprising ease and without even a hint of the sort of arthritic creaking that poetic license would usually attribute to such doors. A bell rang from far off, but no proprietor appeared, nor would one ever materialise, although Andre imagined that a man, whiskered and sagacious of manner, hid in the shadows and watched. Feeling like a head of state visiting the nameless graves of the warfallen, Andre walked between the books. He ran his fingers over their spines; he swept the dust from the gilt-edged pages. Two of the titles caught his attention.

The End

Love Will Pass

There was, he felt, a certain reverence expected of him, and so it was with the stooped posture that is neither a bow nor the upright sort of stance that might seem to denote a lack of care or empathy, that he ventured carefully through the passageways between the thick and thin volumes. The grass was soft beneath his feet, the earth as receptive as flesh. His city shoes were soon made damp and dirtied.

"No author names. No author names… because… because…because… "

And turn, Andre Guillermo, turn. Turn the corner.

"…there are no author names because…"

Yes? Go on. *Go on!*

"…the writers were never acknowledged as authors because… "

He's got it. He knows.

IX
L'OMBRE
matriarch, villainess, mistress

There'd been a shadow following Andre Guillermo most of his life. It was a shadow cast by something that was always out of sight, something that was present but just beyond the reach of his peripheral vision. It was not a black cloud, though some who knew him, but knew nothing of such shadows, would have described it that way. These people said he had a dark side, which the cloud that wasn't a cloud was responsible for.

Whatever people said of the shadow, Andre felt it was a comfort to have it there. It was a constant, and although elusive, it offered succour of the sort found in a mother's embrace, or the sensual black sanctuary gained from burying one's face into a lover's hair. It was both matriarch and mistress. It was, inversely, a storm that offered shelter from the dull calm of dreary days. Andre always thought of the shadow as female, as protective and yet he felt protective of it, and insulted on its behalf whenever people, the people who didn't know him but thought they did, said he was having a black dog day. He didn't like that this ethereal companion of his had a villainess's reputation. He liked to think the shadow that guarded him was that of a raven. Black Dog indeed! Andre had used to like to think he was the sort of man who would never visit the Avenue of Regrettable Farewells. He had forgotten that he'd already been there, years before, when he was a very young man, so young as to have not quite earned the title of man. Fifteen years old.

"A child, Andre," his mother had said. "You are but a child. Save the pains of manhood for when you are one."

X
LA TROISIÈME FENÊTRE REVISITÉ

Andre Guillermo understood. "The writers were never acknowledged as authors because they didn't finish writing their books," he said. Why? Why didn't they finish writing their books "Why? Why didn't they finish writing their books?" Andre repeated the Avenue's words without knowing he'd heard them. Why didn't you finish writing yours, Andre Guillermo?

The Avenue of Regrettable Farewells knows everything.

"I just gave up. They just gave up."

They just gave up? You mean they turned to grey. Grey as a graveyard. A graveyard of unfinished books. Cimetière Des Livres Inachevés.

Welcome back to the Avenue of Regrettable Farewells, Andre Guillermo. Welcome back. It's been a long time.

The book that sat solo on the shelf was called, appropriately, *The Avenue.* This was the book Andre Guillermo most wanted to read. But he would not pick it up or look inside it, not yet, and had he tried to he'd have found the book resisted his attempts to open it, even if it hadn't, he'd have found the book to be made up almost entirely of blank pages.

XI
LA QUATRIÈME FENÊTRE
of calendars and clocks

A calendar sat in the window of the fourth shop. It was a large elaborate version of an old style desk calendar, the type in which the day of the week, the day's number and the month can been seen through little windows. There was a brass dial on one side of it, the purpose of this small wheel, had the calendar been an ordinary one, would be to adjust the date. Here, on the Avenue of Regrettable Farewells the wheel had no such logical function, although it did turn, of its own free will every few seconds, and the little windows blinked like eyes, and its mechanism clicked and ticked. It was the sound a clock's heart makes when it's gone irrevocably mad. In the calendar's windows, instead of the more usual combination of day/month/year, was only the following configuration, which was shown repeatedly, with every revolution of the little brass wheel:

YESTERDAY IS GONE

There were more calendars, none featured any date or time period that was recognisable. One, a standard ring bound paper affair, flipped its pages and as it did, the turning leaves burned before what was written on them, in an ink as burnished and umber as autumn, could be read. A long case clock was behaving very oddly. Its face was not entirely that of a clock, nor completely that of a human, but it had elements that paid a macabre homage to both. It had three escutcheons, as would a timepiece that chimed Westminster style, and these gave the bland ivory plate two unlooking eyes and a small exclamation of a mouth. In the right eyehole sat a key which turned anti-clockwise, and as it did a tear ran down the face and made its way down the clock's case to its base where, in grim reference to an old rhyme, the carcass of a mouse rotted. Several hour glasses, shattered and sandless, lay in the ash fallout created by the eternally burning calendar and from nowhere came a telephone voice, a voice personal yet familiarly generic, that said, This is your alarm call, This is your alarm call, This is your alarm call, over and over and over again.

Andre Guillermo didn't wear a watch. The bag on his back felt suddenly heavier.

XII
GIRL

Andre Guillermo's mother had said, "You are but a child, save the pains of manhood for when you are one. And for the sake of heaven and all that is good, come out from under that black cloud, child."

The raven shadow, present from his youth.

When Andre Guillermo had been fifteen he had loved a girl who loved him back. Man's heart in a boy's body. In later life, once he had become a man, he would say the girl had been a woman, for she'd had, even though she'd only been a year and a whisper older than he, something of woman about her, even then.

In his first letter to the girl, Andre, who was twelve years old at the time, had written:

I like building things and reading and running and climbing and knowing things that other boys don't know. On Saturdays I'm allowed to stay up late. My favourite food is chocolate.

The latter was not true, but he believed girls liked chocolate and wanted to suggest he and this particular girl had something in common. He'd signed off, in a careful but boisterous childman's hand:

I have never written to a girl before. I hope you're not one of those that cries at insects because I like them. Please write back if you don't mind having a boy for a penfriend.

Andre Guillermo

And that was where this story, this story with no end, yet, this story within a story, began...

The girl would include a snapshot of her nubile thirteen-year-old self along with the reply she would write this new penpal boy of hers, this Andre Guillermo. In the photograph she looked moody and awkward, but she told Andre her mother said it was a nice one of her lovely long hair. As if a boy like you who likes reading and running and climbing and knowing things that other boys don't know would notice such things or care about them, wrote the girl, who was a million years old in wit and sensibility.

"I expect her mother teaches mathematics," said Andre Guillermo's mother, on account of the red pen and the graph paper, with which and upon which, respectively, the girl had written. She went on, "At least from that we can assure ourselves that this Juliana comes from a respectable background." It was the first, and would be the last, time Andre's mother ever referred to the girl by name. But it was a name he would whisper for years. And because in reality only he had the intimacy of her name in his mouth, in this story she shall be referred to only as 'the girl'.

And so the years went on, lived out in letters, and when the girl was sixteen she had her hair cut off. She sent a picture of herself to Andre who wrote back saying she looked like a famous film star, the sort who smoked, and that he'd shown the picture to his friend who was jealous but admitted, with a bitter sort of reluctance, that the she was 'toothsome'. In response, the girl wrote back to say her mother disapproved of the new haircut, and had said it looked tawdry and that it was too old for her. And the black clothes she had recently started to wear made her 'look morbid, like a tired Parisian', her mother said, adding that she had used to be 'such a pretty little thing'.

Andre and the girl wrote once a week, sometimes more, and then the letters would overlap in the post. Inevitably she declared love, one that to her felt and was very real. And Andre Guillermo declared love back. He later mused, this young love, tender though it was in its infancy, was possibly more real and of more merit than other loves, because it had grown, at first, from a meeting of minds. He had heard people say that the brain was a sexual organ, or something like that, and he imagined his own snugged in the safety of his skull, throbbing, glistening with the secret thoughts he had begun lately to harbour about the girl. He imagined the girl's pubic hair had grown to form a soft thicket that hid her mute, as yet, he assumed, unkissed lips.

Andre wrote and told her he had been having dreams about her, divine *rêve érotique*, and that he'd been given a thesaurus for Christmas because his mother said he must have used up every word he knew writing all these letters and it was time to expand his vocabulary. In the same letter he wrote that he wanted to feel the 'fecundity' of the girl's body. As always, he signed the letter with his name, and kisses that must be counted, but this time postscripted it with a Shrödinger quote that seemed to the girl when she read it, to have no bearing on anything else in the letter that she could see.

> **"What we observe as material bodies and forces are nothing but shapes and variations in the structure of space."**

You must have been given an encyclopaedia or a book of quotes for Christmas as well as a thesaurus, wrote the girl in response. *At least I hope so. If not, if you just understand and know all these clever things, then you are racing away from me!*

But it would not be the girl's fears of losing ground behind Andre's racing intellect that would result in her losing him and in him losing her. It would be something else entirely, something crueller than any natural close could ever have been. There would never be a natural close, but an enforced end would come and was near, and it would be because of this imposed and painful finish that Andre Guillermo would pay his first visit to the Avenue of Regrettable Farewells. And because both the loss of his love and the visit itself were to be the most agonising experiences the boy had experienced so far, he would choose to shut down his feelings and later choose to forget he had ever been to the Avenue at all. But not before he had given, willingly, his virginity to the girl who was a woman. The girl with the million year old's wit and sensibilities.

XIII
LA CINQUIÈME FENÊTRE
of broken hearts and glass

Several things were unusual about the fifth shop window Andre Guillermo stopped at. The first was that it seemed to be wet with a mist of rain, when none of the other shop windows had been, and there was no sign of rain having fallen recently on The Avenue of Regrettable Farewells. The pavements were dry, the rooftops likewise, and there was no drip-drip from the branches of the trees or from the gutterings of the shops. The second thing that struck Andre as unusual was that in the dewy film that coated the glass someone had marked a rudimentary heart shape with their finger. It was the sort of heart shape the lovestruck young might carve into the barks of trees or inscribe in ink on desktops. The third oddity was that through this heart a break in the glass ran, a jagged and incongruous angled crack that halved the heart and made it two pieces separated, rather than one thing, whole.

It was the first time since arriving at the Avenue of Regrettable Farewells that Andre Guillermo had the notion that anyone had been there before he had. But someone must have been, to have described the heart that would later be broken, on the pane of glass.

"Who was here before I was?" he asked. "Who drew this heart in the raindrops? Who cracked the glass and broke it?" Andre Guillermo was quite convinced that the simple symbol had been drawn before the crack in the glass had been made. And in fairness to him, his logic was not to be questioned. A heart must exist before it can be broken, surely? Although he had been to the Avenue of Regrettable Farewells many years before, he had forgotten ever having been there and so forgotten that logical thinking sometimes took one further from answers or from the solving of mysteries, than not thinking at all.

The Avenue lets a man discover its ways not through learning or deduction, but through feeling, or being. But Andre Guillermo was a thinker. He had been a boy who wanted to know things other boys didn't know, he was now a man who wanted clarity, answers. He wanted to know things other men didn't know, he also wanted to know things other men apparently did know. He wanted to know how best to turn grey, to lose himself in the vast city, to become part of it, to reap its apparent or supposed rewards.

And he wanted to know and understand other things too, things like, how the woman who said she loved him, the woman who had knelt before him in the green garden could love him, when she knew in her heart he couldn't ever be truly free to love her back. He wanted to know why she loved him the way she did. But only she knew that.

Andre Guillermo wiped the glass with his hand, to clear the window for better viewing of the shop's interior. Inside: a scene not unlike that of a study, yet unlike any study he had seen or imagined.

Centred in the scene sat a mahogany escritoire, it stood on inverted pyramidical legs, boasted gilt bronze accenting; and on its platform of Verte de Mer marble sat a bank of small drawers from which a dark fluid leaked, not the blue black of common modern inks, but the blood brown of old. The longest of these drawers drew itself open every few minutes, and upon doing so released a spill of pen nibs which scittered like insects onto the surface of the desk. Some of these nibs pecked at the desk's top, or at the scroll of unwritten parchment that unrolled itself to greet them. One calligraphic beak would dance awhile with the flight feather of a bird, until the two objects fused to make a quill as sharp and intentful as an arrow, that wrote in an ink that came from no well or pot but came from its simply having become a pen. It wrote two words, repeatedly, on the paper.

Dear John, Dear John, Dear John, Dear John, Dear John, Dear John, Dear John, Dear John, Dear John…

The Avenue of Regrettable Farewells is a trickster. Things become animate, are driven not by hands but by will, by memory, things are haunted by the ghosts of goodbye. Machines are possessed, objects are imbued with life by that most aching of feelings – regret. The turning of wheels, the ticking of clocks, the dull harmony dial tone of a Bakelite phone. There is a ghost town mood and the lights are dimmed to mourn sentiments and dreams dead or killed, or simply hopes that seemingly can never be fulfilled.

XIV
LE MUR D'ADIEUX DANS TOUTES LES LANGUES
of silence and stone

On a wall like a death wall, like a list of those fallen in war, inscribed in stone, the word goodbye, in every tongue ever known to the Avenue, and sometimes in tongues not understood. Untranslatable tongues. Occasionally there is simply a graven tear – for not everyone can say goodbye in words. And you can't carve silence into stone.

XV
LETTRES ÉCRITES
EN LARMES

of dried tears rewet with a boy's weeping

When the girl was taken on vacation by her parents she sent postcards to Andre, as promised. These bright pictorial greetings came from vibrant places, places where ripe succulent fruits oozed a sort of sexy allure from their taut skins and dark deft-fingered gypsy men shook fists full of silver on beaches with equally silvery sands. The girl didn't mention being in love with him, or out of it, and this lack of expression came, Andre assumed, from the open nature of the postcards and the idea that the girl's parents would read them. She didn't mention love again, not for a while, but she did sign the cards with an elaborate artistic X for a kiss. Andre noticed that her handwriting had become more that of a woman than of a girl. The strokes were bold, confident and written, he imagined, by a hand that could very easily caress him to ecstasy and that must, hopefully when thinking of him, adeptly enjoy private pleasures. He liked to think that with thoughts of him the girl fell prey to an almost torturous rise of delight and desire.

Over the years Andre's mother had read every letter that arrived for her son, and it was the same with these postcards. Once, Andre had tried to put his foot down, but his mother was not to be thwarted, though she feigned indifference and said she wasn't really interested in the sort of balderdash silly young things with derision and told Andre to stop mooning about. The word 'balderdash' had ejaculated from her mouth like shot.

Andre Guillermo had not lost his virginity. He had given it willingly and defiantly, gift that it was, to the girl who had given her his. She had returned from vacation with a worldliness and something of the exotic exuding from her. The how and why doesn't not matter. The details of which trains they caught, of the address of the rendezvous, or even the date are of no consequence. All that need be known is that it happened, as it was meant to and was destined to. Secretly.

For some time this business between Andre and the girl had been viewed as dangerous by both families, there had been every attempt to put a stop to what had become known as 'the whole ridiculous affair'. The girl's mother was not a maths teacher, as his mother had decided. Her mother was, as was his, a woman who wished to protect her child from the apparent perils of loving too young, of feeling too much, of being too intense, of being 'all-taken-up-with-things'.

Steps would be taken.

One love had sent them all mad it seemed, all except Andre and the girl who had no fear of love at all, only a fear of losing it, of being denied it, of having it taken from them. And soon, of course, it would be taken from them. The families agreed. This must stop. It was to be the end of days. It was to be Andre Guillermo's first experience of a truly regrettable farewell.

"Anyway," said Andre Guillermo's mother tutting to the skies, "it isn't real love. The boy is too young to know real love."

Andre's sisters laughed. They laughed at their mother for her habit of talking to the heavens as if some God were watching, and listening. They laughed at the tearstained letters the girl subsequently sent Andre, at the declarations of ardour, the claims of a broken unmendable heart.

They laughed at the way their brother counted the inked kisses and kissed the girl's dried tears and rewet them into life with his own weeping. They laughed because when they saw their mother shooing an invisible raven away. They laughed because she herself seemed as flappy as a crazed bird that was as much a shadow to her son as the imagined cloud.

"Off with you," she demanded, "Be gone, foul cloud!" she cried to the shadow that was not a shadow.

But the shadow, it seemed, was not to be deterred. It had fixed Andre in its sights. Where he went, so it went. As he walked, so it flew.

A boy like the young Andre Guillermo may fuck as brutally hard and as sweetly, tenderly, as a fully formed man, but he is still a boy. He may fight like a champion, thumping rule straight noses out of line, bloodying them, flooring other boys, boys by the docks with smileless eyes and snarls as names. But he's still a boy. He is his sisters' darling little plaything, a toy that never breaks. He is his mother's child. His heart may be irrevocably stitched and in part eternally bound to his sweetheart's. His eyes may see nothing but her imagined face on closing. His cock may have been in the silent mouth and the secret core of her, his cum might have spilled in her throat or her cunt, but his destiny is, for that cruel flash of time that is his fledglinghood, entirely in his mother's hands.

XVI
LA SALLE DANS L'HÔTEL

of a marionette and
memories misremembered

Andre Guillermo found himself in a small room which he understood to have been long abandoned. There was a tatter of floral silk at the window that was so decayed it had only the faintest description of its once-red overblown roses left; he saw these ashen rouged shadows and thought of lipsticked ghost kisses printed on the rim of a crystal glass or echo-smeared on a lace-edged handkerchief. On a side table, clean crisp ivory sheets of crested notepaper.

L'Hôtel

The Avenue of Regrettable Farewells

There was a washstand with rust marks on its tiled top and here sat a jug and a bowl, both brim-filled with a water so clean as to be pure as weeping - it would, Andre mused, have been a sin to wash with it. He drank some from the jug though, and as he drank, thirsted more, and yet the pitcher never ran dry, it simply re-filled itself to fulfil his need.

There was a bed, large enough to sleep one, that had ribbons and dried flowers and garlands of grasses tied to its metal stead and a mattress with ochred ticking. On the window sill a dead moth sat like a newly placed flower on a grave. Despite death it was still vibrant in colour and more starkly illustrated against the scattered crumbs of frass and the cracked and stained paintwork of the sill. This was a room of unbreathing rather than a room of death, yet all things within it were lifeless, except the water which now flowed from the jug's petulant lip and spilled out from the bowl's rim over the top of the washstand and onto the wooden floor. Andre thought, To be lifeless is not the same as being dead. He surprised himself by thinking he must find out what type the moth was when he returned to what he supposed was reality, or waking life, or that other world. That world of grey, that city, that place which was not The Avenue of Regrettable Farewells. He had never seen a moth like this one: soot black with red-tipped wings, like a bloodsucker faerie. He wanted its long Latin name on his tongue. He wanted anything on his tongue but the addictive nectar he had just drunk. He feared it, feared how it seemed to have been designed for him, how it both quenched and unquenched him, how in sipping once he risked being possessed by the need for an eternal supply of it.

He knew the yellowed mattress would

feel damp, but he sat on the bed anyway. It was now he saw the cupboard with its slightly open door. He hadn't noticed it before, perhaps it had not been there until now, this dreamscape town was odd like that, things shifted, disappeared or were magickally conjured from nowhere.

Andre found the slightly open cupboard door both alluring and sinister. If he'd been a child, sleeping in that bed, he'd have been unable to settle without shutting the door first.

A voice said, "Open the door." It was a woman's voice, a deep persuasive voice, and it came, Andre thought, from beyond the door and elsewhere. "Please," it said, whispering now and less in command of itself. Andre thought he could hear tears, or at least the slight tremor that might precede them. He stood, feeling weightless, and walked to the cupboard. He was aware now of being barefoot suddenly but could not recall if he had been so upon entering the room. Actually, he had no recollection of getting to the room, or the building that it was a part of. He just recalled finding himself in it and this experience commencing from that point. As if nothing had existed before this either in his waking life or any dream he'd ever had. The wet wooden floor felt inexplicably warm beneath his bare feet and with each step he took toward the cupboard the floor yielded underfoot, as if made from a substance other than wood, something softer, something moist, giving, something that smelled of every freshly-broken morning he had known as a boy and as a man. Grass. Just as the floor of the bookshop that was not a bookshop had been of earth and graveyard grass, this room too grew its own garden. Between the cracks in the floorboards fine green cilia had sprouted and upshot itself to maturity and an instant lush field stretched before him; tall stems of vivid buttercups and cornflowers swayed in a breeze that came from where the window had once been. Behind him, the bed was no longer a bed, but a beast with ornate horns black as iron and slicked dark with oil or meadow dew. He was conscious of what lay behind him without turning to look. The animal wore the garlands that had bedecked the bed, as if it were thought sacred and had been adorned by believers who believed such could be sacrosanct. Only the cupboard door remained unchanged in this shifting scene. It stood, a Ruth in a corn field, isolated against the backdrop of the eternally dancing flowers and a sudden watercolour-wash sky that bled out clouds and golden sunrays.

Andre walked forever and for no time at all and reaching the cupboard, curled his fingers around the door handle - there appeared to be something snakelike in its design which, when he look more closely, turned slowly to a metal vine that wrapped itself around his wrist then faded and was nothing more than a plain tarnished brass handle again when he blinked. The briefest of handfastings.

"Please," the voice said, again.

The door opened soundlessly and there she was – in darkness; the marionette, hanged in her russet-apocalypse gown of tawny golds, like a cock pheasant in a pantry, or an unripe browning pear, wasp-sexed but not yet stung enough or dead enough to fall from the branch. Upside down. Strung up by the footstrings on a rusted hook, in a cubby that was close and intimate and shady and yet vast, unending, leading nowhere and off to infinity. Her legs, bound as they were, described a modesty she could not, inhuman as she was, possibly feel or know. But it was not to the blackstained hollow between them that Andre's eye was drawn, it was to the thunderbolt of jet hair that shot in choppy waving tresses to the floor from beneath her upturned dress. Without touching it, he knew this tumbling bolt of silken shadow to be human hair, despite the body of the marionette being so obviously some sort of composite on wood.

The idea of untying her came from his rational mind, it was perhaps what she wanted, why she had called him to the cupboard in the first place, her reason for whispering that desperate plea to him in that tremulous voice. In an everyday situation he might have succumbed to rationale, to the conventional rule of acting logically, and immediately, gallantly, released her from her undignified topsy-turvy state of imprisonment. But this was unwaking nightless night, and the wakening-sleeping-dreaming-dream man of him was more a creature of instinct. He wanted to see her face. He liked faces. He was a man for whom pornography regularly failed – if he couldn't find a particular something in a face he derived only the wrong sort of unsatisfying guilty enjoyment in masturbating over a body he felt merely a shallow kind of craving for.It was usually a certain look in the eyes that attracted him, not the pseudo smouldering look accompanied by a bloated pout that women and nubile girls adopted these days, but something else. The sign of a word maybe, a sigil, or even the entire lack of a pupil or iris and only the reflection of his own self found there in place of them. He liked, longed for, he supposed, a woman who didn't just look at him, but saw him. One in whose eyes he would see and know himself.

As he reached out his hand to touch that stormfall of hair he found he couldn't – as the dream mutes the mouth and prevents the screamer from screaming for help it also, sometimes, stills the limbs and stops the man who wants to run from danger from running from it, or the girl who wants to walk away defiant from taking even a single indignant step in those shoes her mother disapproved of but wickedly wore herself. The dream stops the mother safety-netting her eager arms beneath the infant who plummets to a death more certain than any hope of living. Dreams both stop and start us. The Avenue of Regrettable Farewells knows this.

When Andre did finally touch the marionette it was in a way that was both decorous and starkly intimate. He lifted the inside-out, upturned-skirts upandover her legs, covering the knotted pine hollow of her cuntless thicketless crotch, to reveal her face.

Here: A life lesson in a death mask. The eyes were painted shut but the mouth was carved open. The cavity beyond the full rumcherry lacquered lips was blacked with shade and lack of human blood or tongue, and so deep was it that Andre thought for a moment that within that cavern there might be another marionette strung ungainly on another hook and so on, and so on and on and on and on…

And on again…

An so on…

Remember, here on the Avenue of Regrettable Farewells all things are in a state of aimless perpetuality; no journeys seem to conclude, not a single destination is ever reached, and so a pointless termite's purpose is as lost as a lost person's. All non-culminating experience is captured.

In putting his finger in the mouth's darkness he felt the unwomanliness of the puppet, yet still thought of this strange 'it' affectionately, as 'her'. He could feel the threads, the carvings of her, felt the lines and ridges formed by something mechanical and harder than wood and imagined a powerful drill bit, cock-shaped and hammering, into the wood of her face before her face had even been a face, determinedly, rhythmically fucking out the centred gape that would be, eventually, her supposedly talkless mouth. It was this image that, imagined in a dream still being dreamed, in a story that was writing itself as it was told, that damped the dream and made it moist and sexually charged, if not yet entirely wet.

He wondered what dead tree the timber of her had been cut from and if in the forest that was now bereft of it there lay a scar in the ground in the shape of a woman or a stump in the form of a heart broken, sliced through. He tucked the hem of her skirts into the strings that tangled her ankles together and she transformed from pheasant or fruit and was now chrysalisic, cocooned in her own decayed finery, still hanged there waiting to either hatch or be cut free. She was a fly in a web, she was insectoid in so many ways he almost felt her buzz when she whispered, "Please," again. This time the threat of crying had entirely vanished from her voice and there was a distinct tone of seduction in it. In reaching up to unhook the marionette from her indignity Andre found himself pressed against her body. His face rested in the folds of earthy silks that now hid her wooden mound. He breathed deep, then deeper, shocked to find that there was something human about the scent of her. He felt his clothes fade and his naked cock rise and butt involuntarily against her oblivious face. Let loose she folded and slipped softly to the ground and lay there, eyes closed in that constant state of repose at his bare feet. Blind fallen Magdalene to a naked roused Christ. A drop of the water, which still shimmered and rippled like a melted silver moon on the floor, found its way onto her cheek and she reclined there, lachrymose, unmoving, his.

"Don't cry," Andre said, and immediately wanted her to. "Cry, do cry," he said. Andre was surprised to hear that his voice was the voice he used in every day life. This didn't fit his idea of the dream man he dreamed he was. He'd envisioned himself with long blond hair; something which for some reason he felt showed his true being. "I've missed you," he said. "I've missed you forever." He thought he heard her say, "I love your voice." This was because she had, and she did. She always would.

Think not of this man, of Andre Guillermo, as some terrible thoughtless philanderer, or a Casanova of our modern times. Think of him, only, as a well he hasn't yet wished his own coin into. Or a star as yet unwished upon. Yes, he loved a girl. He loves his wife. He loves a woman. It is almost as if these three appear as cameos, a triptych made up of very different witches, in the love and the life of him.

At this stage in the story Andre Guillermo is a man carrying the burden of the love he lost. The girl. And the burden of the love he later loved and still loves. His wife. Add to this the terrible weight and guilt of wanting a love he is yet to fully be free to love. The woman.

But it was not these three that had hold of him as he wandered back to the bookshop that was not a bookshop on the Avenue of Regrettable Farewells.

When a man is away from his women, he is man alone, and nothing more. He went back to the bookshop.

He didn't know why he did. But we do.

XVII
RETOUR AU CIMETIÈRE DES LIVRES INACHEVÉS

of an untold tale

told in the telling

The book that was previously titled *The End* was now titled *The Endeavour* and the book called *Love Will Pass* now bore the words *Love Will Passion Bring* upon its spine. Andre thought he would like one day to read these books, but it was still the book called *The Avenue* that he wished most to read. And yet, although it was a desire to read that seemed to govern him, he found in his hand a pen of the type he had seen earlier. The calligraphic beak adjoined to the flight feather of a bird, these two objects fused to make a quill as sharp and intentful as an arrow. The pen, or rather, the man, wrote in an ink that came from no well or pot but came from him simply having realised he had long become a man, but was yet to become the writer he knew he could be. And he found, as the feathered thing vibrated and sputted out its dark ejaculate that he was tracing the nib of the tool over the book's title, making it clearer. Writing…

THE AVENUE

And then, when the words seemed to have settled themselves and become his, he added to them…

THE AVENUE OF REGRET
then…

**THE AVENUE OF
REGRETTABLE FARE**

Regrettable fare! He thought suddenly of an under-par scallop that had rendered him sick for days, and then remembered that this had just been something he had imagined, a lie he had told as a means to take a much needed day away from his job in the City of Grey. In the grey world of grey days, grey modern people called this 'pulling a sicky'. He laughed. He would finish the title. In this thick thumping thunderous ink that now flowed like feeling… He wrote:

THE
AVENUE
OF
REGRETTABLE
FAREWELLS

And the book opened, quite of its own accord and in accordance with him. Pages like the legs of a lover, spread, inviting. Each page headed with:

L'Hôtel

The Avenue of Regrettable Farewells

Andre Guillermo began to write… at least he thought he began to write; really he was only tracing words he'd already written. But that was and is what the avenue is for, to let us retrace steps we have taken and steps we have fallen down, flights of stairs and even fancy, even our missed steps, steps trodden out of time with the world. He wrote as if the words were entirely new to him:

"The Avenue of Regrettable Farewells is situated beyond a corner as yet unturned. A corner of a street; a street that is, in its mad fusion of brazen modern attitude and ancient architecture, much like any other street that houses shops whose windows offer untold treasures for strangely shaped and even ill-gotten coins. Technically, it might be supposed, the 'street' out of which the 'avenue' runs tributary, is more an avenue than the avenue itself, but where myth and whispers and the aches of hearts govern, there is no place for technicality. And as this avenue, this living graveyard of goodbyes, boasts no postal address and claims no place on any geographical map, it can be named

an avenue or a lane or whatsoever it or anyone, for that matter, wishes; for who can dispute the details of that which does not exist for everyone and does not, when it does exist, manifest itself in identical ways in the eyes of the beholders? The avenue, like beauty, is indefinable. Like love, it is intangible. Like death, it is just around a corner as yet unturned..."

Hour upon hour and yet in no time at all, he filled the almost blank pages, and when he reached the last one and wrote the last words and signed his name he marvelled that the book had seemed to know when he would finish before he did.

Andre Guillermo closed the book and put it, along with the quill, in his overnight bag, the one filled with the dreams he had brought with him, dreams he had intended to rid himself of. Oddly, the bag seemed lighter, less burdensome, despite the fact that he hadn't discarded any of its contents and despite the fact that it appeared there were new dreams in it now. He could see his reflection, golden, in the golden sheen of these new dreams. He zipped up the bag, buckled it tight and lifted it onto his back and he wandered slowly back down the Avenue of Regrettable Farewells. He didn't look at anything in particular, because he thought he had seen it all. But in passing a shop he'd forgotten he'd passed before, he noticed that a boy knelt outside it weeping. And as the boy cried, on and on, the glass in the window wetted itself in recognition of his very real grief, and the window steamed as if angry, with rain. And the boy tried to wipe the tears from the glass, but in doing so found he couldn't, and he drew there, with his finger, a heartshape. It was the sort of heartshape the lovestruck young might carve into the barks of trees or inscribe in ink on desktops.

Andre Guillermo watched as the boy then broke the glass and the heart with a hearty punch. And he thought, A heart must exist before it is broken and he waved at the boy, and the boy waved back.

Remember, Andre Guillermo had forgotten he had ever been to the Avenue of Regrettable Farewells. It had been such a long time, he didn't even recognise himself.

Even so, he had turned many a corner and would turn another corner now. But he didn't turn grey. He rounded the corner that led him out of the mysterious avenue and into, or onto, a street. It was a street in a city. It could have been your city, or mine, in this country or that – any principal metropolis. The City of Grey.

And Andre Guillermo walked in this grey city, on its graphite pavements, in the beautiful golden shining of its beautiful golden sun. And a raven shadow followed him.

THE END

Venus De Mileage

"We are shaped by our thoughts;
we become what we think.
When the mind is pure,
joy follows like a shadow that never leaves."

Buddha

Printed in Germany
by Amazon Distribution
GmbH, Leipzig